Rushing River

Written by Penny Dolan
Illustrated by Kirsten Richards

WAYLAND

Warwickshire County Council

Hers? / /	0 1 OCT 2015		
1 2 SEP 2011	- 7 NOV 2016		
2 9 FEB 2012	6 SEP 2017		
1 0 JUL 2012	1 5 MAR 2018		
1 8 JUL 2012	2 1 AUG 2019		
2 5 JUL 2012	2 8 OCT 2021		
1 2 SEP 2012			
2 6 NOV 2012			
2 7 FEB 2013			
1 9 FEB 2015			

This item is to be returned or renewed before the latest date above. It may be borrowed for a further period if not in demand. **To renew your books:**

- **Phone the 24/7 Renewal Line 01926 499273 or**
- **Visit www.warwickshire.gov.uk/libraries**

Discover • Imagine • Learn • *with libraries*

Warwickshire County Council

Working for Warwickshire

First published in 2009
by Wayland

This paperback edition published in 2010 by Wayland

Text copyright © Penny Dolan 2009
Illustration copyright © Kirsten Richards 2009

Wayland
338 Euston Road
London NW1 3BH

Wayland Australia
Level 17/207 Kent Street
Sydney, NSW 2000

Series Editor: Louise John
Editor: Katie Powell
Cover design: Paul Cherrill
Design: D.R.ink
Consultant: Shirley Bickler

A CIP catalogue record for this book is available from the British Library.

ISBN 9780750257398 (hbk)
ISBN 9780750260367 (pbk)

Printed in China

Wayland is a division of Hachette Children's Books,
an Hachette UK Company

www.hachette.co.uk

The family were walking through
the forest, searching for a place to
set up camp.
"Here we are," said Pa, at last.

Ma began to make a shelter from animal
skins and branches. Erg and his sister,
Luli, collected some wood for the fire.

"I recognise this spot!" cried Luli. "It was autumn and the leaves on the trees were yellow the last time we came here."

"Yes," said Erg. "I remember this was a good place to hunt for food, too."

"Can you find your way to the river bank?" asked Ma.
"I think so," said Luli. Erg nodded.

"Go and fetch some water," said Ma, and she handed Luli a thick brown sack made from animal skin.

"Don't go near the deep water!" Ma called, as Luli and Erg ran off laughing.

The children padded carefully through the trees. It was hard to remember the way to the river.

"All these paths look the same," said Erg.

Just then, Luli stopped.
"Listen!" she cried. "I can hear
the sound of rushing water."

"The river must be that way," said Erg.
"Come on! I think we can take a
short cut."

They pushed through the trees, and
came out at the top of a steep bank.
The river below them glinted and shone
in the sunlight.

"Luli, that's not just the water shining," cried Erg, pointing to the rippling water.

"It's fish! Lots and lots of leaping fish!" gasped Luli.

The children started dancing about on
the steep bank. Fish meant food! Fish
meant feasts!

But the bank was wet and muddy.
Suddenly, Erg slipped down
towards the water.

Luli reached out to stop him falling,
but she started to slip, too.

Down, down they tumbled, right into
the deepest part of the river.

"Quick, grab the grass," shouted Luli, but the tufts of grass were so wet that they slipped straight through their hands.

"Hold onto those branches up there!" cried Erg, but the thin twigs just snapped.

The children gasped for breath as they bobbed underneath the water, and fought their way to the surface again.

The current was strong and it soon swept the struggling children along.

When a log came floating by, the children grabbed it.

Luli tried to climb up on top of it, but the log rolled right over, and then drifted away from her.

The only thing the children could cling on to was their floating water sack.

"Oh, no! There's a waterfall coming up!"
shouted Erg.

"Help! Help!" Luli cried. "Erg, what shall
we do?"

"Erg? Luli?" Someone was calling out their names. It was Pa. He was standing with Grandpa and a group of men on the bank scanning the water for fish.

"Here's two very funny fish!" he shouted.

The strong men lifted Luli and Erg out of the water.

The children hugged Pa tightly, crying with relief.

Grandpa took Luli and Erg straight
back to the family's camp.
"The fire will soon dry you off," he said.
"The water in that river is freezing."

Ma ran towards them as they neared
the camp.

"You two must take more care," Ma scolded, but she was very relieved to see them.

"Did you get any fresh water during your big adventure?" she asked.

"I don't think so," Luli said,
and she held up the water sack.
"What's that?" Ma gasped.

Luli looked down and saw that the
water sack was twisting and turning.

"It's a monster," shouted Erg.
Luli dropped the sack and out slipped
an enormous fish.

"That's a monster all right," laughed
Ma. "Just wait 'till your Pa sees what
you've caught. We'll have a good
supper tonight!"

That evening, Luli and Erg gathered around the big fire. They watched their fish cook over the hot ashes.

"Eat well, you two," said Pa. "Tomorrow you have something important to do."

"What's that?" asked Luli and Erg, puzzled.

"Tomorrow I am taking you back to the river," said Pa.

"To catch fish?" asked Erg.

"You caught fish well enough today," laughed Pa. "Tomorrow you are going to learn how to swim!"

START READING is a series of highly enjoyable books for beginner readers. **The books have been carefully graded to match the Book Bands widely used in schools.** This enables readers to be sure they choose books that match their own reading ability.

Look out for the Band colour on the book in our Start Reading logo.

The Bands are:

Pink Band 1A & 1B

Red Band 2

Yellow Band 3

Blue Band 4

Green Band 5

Orange Band 6

Turquoise Band 7

Purple Band 8

Gold Band 9

START READING books can be read independently or shared with an adult. They promote the enjoyment of reading through satisfying stories supported by fun illustrations.

Penny Dolan enjoys writing stories on her computer at home, and sharing stories with children in schools and libraries. Penny also likes reading, painting and playing djembe drums. She has two grown-up children and one bad cat.

Kirsten Richards lives in a small house near Oxford with her two cats, three plants and more spiders than she'd like to contemplate. When freed from her duties of cat food opener and chin scratcher, she draws and paints to her heart's content.